My "h" Sound Box®

Library of Congress Cataloging-in-Publication Data
Moncure, Jane Belk.
My "h" sound box / by Jane Belk Moncure; illustrated by Colin King.
p. cm.
Summary: A little boy fills his sound box with many words beginning with the letter "h."
ISBN 1-56766-774-0 (lib. reinforced : alk. paper)
[1. Alphabet.] I. King, Colin, ill. II. Title.
PZ7.M739 Myh 2000
[E]—dc21   99-056560

My "h" Sound Box

Jane Belk Moncure

illustrated by Colin King

The Child's World®

Little  had a box.

"I will find things that begin
with my 'h' sound," he said.

"I will put them into

my sound box."

He found some hats.

He put a hat on his  head.

Did he put the other hats into the box?

He did.

Little  found a hen.

"Hello," he said. "I need a hen for my sound box." He put the hen into the box with the hats.

Then he found a hog.

Did he put the hog into the box with the hen and the hats?

He did.

Little  h found a horse.

He was happy.
He hopped on
the horse.

He rode the horse up a high hill.

"I want to go higher," said Little . But the horse could not go higher. They were on top of the hill.

So Little

put the horse into the box with the hats, the hen, and the hog.

Now the box was heavy. Little put it on his head.

He did not see the hole.

He hopped into the hole.

"Help! Help!"

"How can we get out of this  hole?"

asked the hen,

the hog,

and the horse.

Little  h had a horn.

"I will blow my horn," he said.

He blew the horn.

A hippopotamus

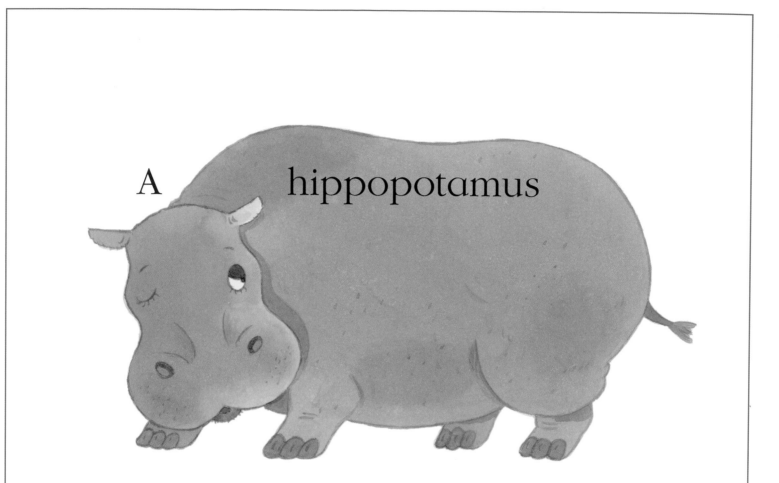

heard the horn.
He helped them out of the hole.

"Hurrah for the hippo!"
everyone hollered.

"How can I thank you for helping us out of the hole?"

asked Little  h.

"You can take me for a ride in the helicopter,"

said the hippopotamus.

So Little  took the helicopter out of the box.

He and all the animals went for a ride.

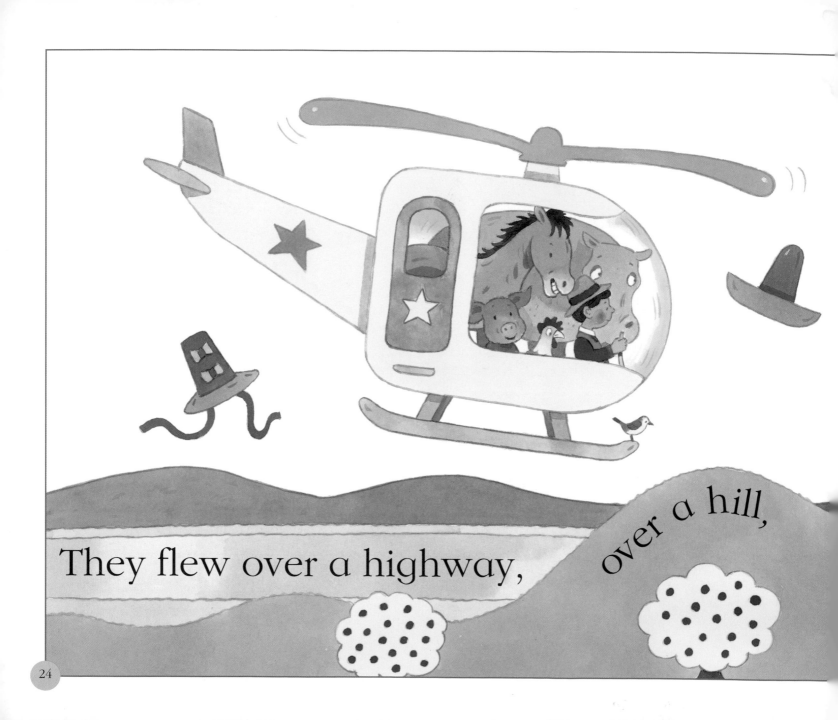

They flew over a highway, over a hill,

and all the way home.

There, Little  h spread out his things.

horn

horse

hen

helicopter

hats

hippopotamus

hog

My! How many he had!

Can you read these words
with Little  ?

hair

hot dog

harp

hand

honey

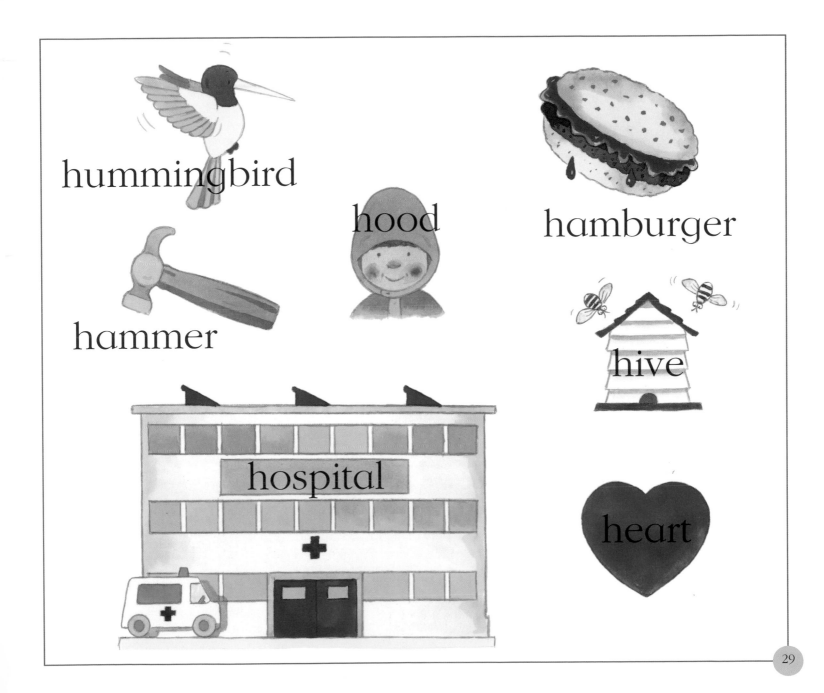

hummingbird

hammer

hood

hamburger

hive

hospital

heart

ABOUT THE AUTHOR AND ILLUSTRATOR

Jane Belk Moncure began her writing career when she was in kindergarten. She has never stopped writing. Many of her children's stories and poems have been published, to the delight of young readers, including her son Jim, whose childhood experiences found their way into many of her books.

Mrs. Moncure's writing is based upon an active career in early childhood education. A recipient of an M.A. degree from Columbia University, Mrs. Moncure has taught and directed nursery, kindergarten, and primary grade programs in California, New York, Virginia, and North Carolina. As a former member of the faculties of Virginia Commonwealth University and the University of Richmond, she taught prospective teachers in early childhood education.

Mrs. Moncure has travelled extensively abroad, studying early childhood programs in the United Kingdom, The Netherlands, and Switzerland. She was the first president of the Virginia Association for Early Childhood Education and received its award for outstanding service to young children.

A resident of North Carolina, Mrs. Moncure is currently a full-time writer and educational consultant. She is married to Dr. James A. Moncure, former vice president of Elon College.

Colin King studied at the Royal College of Art, London. He started his freelance career as an illustrator, working for magazines and advertising agencies.

He began drawing pictures for children's books in 1976 and has illustrated over sixty titles to date.

Included in a wide variety of subjects are a best-selling children's encyclopedia and books about spies and detectives.

His books have been translated into several languages, including Japanese and Hebrew. He has four grown-up children and lives in Suffolk, England, with his wife, three dogs, and a cat.